W9-BSH-658

My Spring Robin

By Anne Rockwell

Pictures by Harlow Rockwell & Lizzy Rockwell

SCHOLASTIC INC.

NEW YORK   TORONTO   LONDON   AUCKLAND   SYDNEY

For Dr. Mike Marino

No part of this publication may be reproduced in whole or in part, or stored in a retrieval system, or transmitted in any form or by any means, electronic, mechanical, photocopying, recording, or otherwise, without written permission of the publisher. For information regarding permission, write to Macmillan Publishing Company, 866 Third Avenue, New York, NY 10022.

ISBN 0-590-46257-1

Text copyright © 1989 by Anne Rockwell.
Illustrations copyright © 1989 by Harlow Rockwell and Lizzy Rockwell.
All rights reserved. Published by Scholastic Inc., 730 Broadway, New York, NY 10003, by arrangement with Macmillan Publishing Company.

12 11 10 9 8 7 6 5 4 3   5 6 7 8/9
Printed in the U.S.A.   08

First Scholastic printing, March 1993

A robin sang a song for me
every day last summer.
I liked that robin.

But in the fall
my robin flew away.
My father said
it would come back
in the spring.
So when spring came,

I went looking for my spring robin.

I saw a bee
taking honey from a crocus,
but I didn't see my robin.

I looked into the yellow forsythia bush,

but my robin wasn't there.

My robin was not sitting
high up in the branches
of the magnolia tree.

In the fern garden
behind our outdoor table,

fuzzy fiddleheads were sprouting
in last year's wet, brown leaves.

But I didn't see
my robin there.

I saw a tiny toad.
It hopped behind
a clump of daffodils
to hide from me.

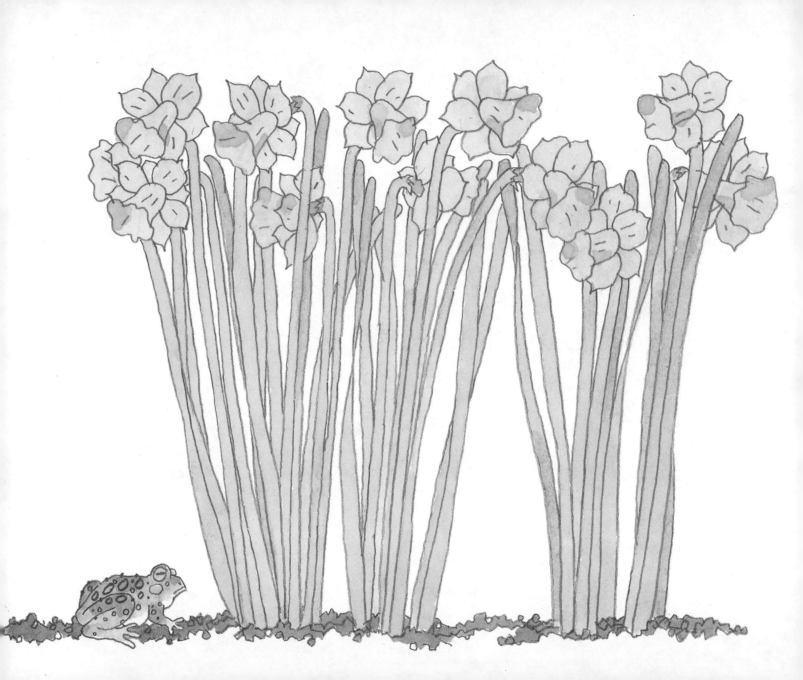

I looked high up into the sky
to see if my robin
was flying back to me.
Drops of rain fell on my face,
and our neighbor's cat ran home.

After the shower I picked
a little bunch of purple violets
for my mother.
I watched a shiny earthworm
wriggle up out of the ground.

And then I heard it.
I heard that song!
"Cheer-up, cheerilee!
Cheer-up, cheerilee!
Cheer-up, cheerilee!"
I knew who was singing that song!

It was my spring robin!